Tedd Arnold

Orchard Books • New York
An Imprint of Scholastic Inc.

Specially for Scott and McKenzie

All rights reserved. Published by Orchard Books, an imprint of Scholastic Inc.,
Publishers since 1920. ORCHARD BOOKS and design are registered trademarks of Watts
Publishing Group, Ltd., used under license. SCHOLASTIC and associated logos are
trademarks and/or registered trademarks of Scholastic Inc.

Library of Congress Cataloging-in-Publication Data

Arnold, Tedd, author, illustrator.
A pet for Fly Guy / Tedd Arnold.
pages cm
Summary: In this first Fly Guy picture book,
Buzz tries to help Fly Guy find the right pet.
ISBN 978-0-545-31615-6
1. Flies—Juvenile fiction. 2. Pets—Juvenile fiction. 3. Humorous stories.
[1. Flies—Fiction. 2. Pets—Fiction. 3. Humorous stories.] I. Title.
PZ7.A7379Pe 2014
813.54—dc23
2013035044

10 9 8 7 6 5 4 3 2 1   14 15 16 17 18

Printed in China   38
First printing, May 2014

The display type was hand-lettered.
The text was set in Hank BT.
The art was created digitally using Photoshop.
Book design by Chelsea C. Donaldson

A boy had a pet fly.
He named him —

FLY GUY!

Fly Guy was the smartest pet
in the world. He could say
the boy's name —

BUZZ!

One day, Buzz said,
"Fly Guy, we are going on a picnic!"

Buzz and Fly Guy played chase all the way to the park.

They ate lunch.
They played together.

They looked at clouds.

They watched other people play with their pets.

"Wow!" said Buzz. "Everyone has a pet."

NO PETZ!

"Oops! That's right," said Buzz.
"You don't have a pet."

"But remember, you have to take care of it," said Buzz.

"And play with it," said Buzz.

"And feed it," said Buzz.

"Okay," said Buzz, "let's go to the pet shop."

At the pet shop, Buzz came out with a puppy.
It licked Fly Guy.

Buzz came out with a kitten.
It swatted Fly Guy.

Buzz came out with a frog.
It chased Fly Guy.

Back at the park, Fly Guy found a worm.
It was too slimy.

Fly Guy found a spider.
It was too tangly.

Fly Guy found a cricket.
It was too jumpy.

Buzz said, "Let's think about this whole pet thing."

"You need a pet who likes to play," said Buzz. "Just like you."

"You need a pet who can do tricks," said Buzz. "Just like you."

"You need a pet who is a good friend," said Buzz.
"Just like you."

"And," said Buzz, "you need a pet with a cool name."

"I never thought of that," said Buzz.
"Okay, sure. I mean, YEZZ!"

"There's just one thing about being your pet," said Buzz.

"You don't have to feed me."

Buzz said, "Do you know who's the best pet in the whole wide world?"